Who's in the Mirror?

Who's in the Mirror?

PHOEBE ERICKSON

ALFRED A. KNOPF　　　NEW YORK

L.C. Catalog card number: 65-11964

This is a Borzoi book, published by Alfred A. Knopf, Inc.

For Avery and Fredrick

Οne day, Bulges Beaver found a small mirror in the tall grass near the pond. He hurried home to show it to his mother.

"See what I found," he said. "When you look into
it, you see a beaver."

His mother took the mirror. "Why yes, it is a beaver.
Isn't that nice," she said.

When Bulges' father looked into the mirror, he said, "What a strong, handsome beaver! I wonder where he lives."

Bulges took the mirror to his friend, Roundly Raccoon.

"What is that?" asked Roundly.

"I don't know," replied Bulges. "But when you look into it, you see a beaver."

"Really? Let me see." Roundly looked into the mirror. "Yipes—a raccoon!"

"It is not! It's a beaver!" shouted Bulges. "I guess I know a beaver when I see one!"

He took the mirror from Roundly and held it at paw's length. "I knew I was right. It *is* a beaver."

"That's not what I saw," replied Roundly. "I saw a raccoon."

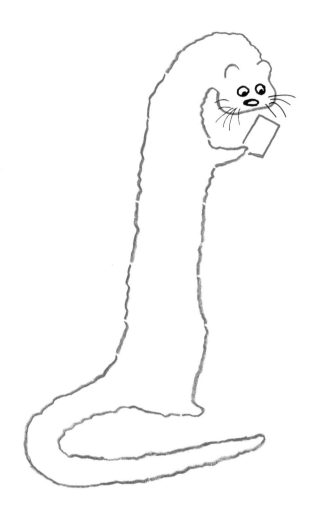

Oddly Otter came along.

"What's all the shouting about?" she asked.

Bulges gave her the mirror. "Look into this and tell us what you see," he said.

Oddly looked—and looked—and looked.

"What do you see?" asked Bulges impatiently.

"Well you won't believe it, but I see the most dreamy otter," replied Oddly.

"Otter!!" shouted Bulges and Roundly at once.

"That's what I said," murmured Oddly, still staring into the mirror.

Roundly shook his head. "Well I never. But anyway, it proves I was right. It isn't a beaver."

"Slowly Bear solves problems," said Oddly. "We'll have to take it to him."

Roundly and Bulges agreed, and the three friends went off together. They walked a long way and at last they found Slowly Bear. He was talking to Putter Porcupine.

"Excuse us, please," said Bulges. "But we have a problem for you to solve."

"You came to the right place," replied Slowly. "I love problems—that is, if they take a long time to solve."

"This one won't," Oddly said.

"Then, I'm not interested," said Slowly.

"I might try it," said Putter. "I sometimes solve problems in my spare time."

"Oh, thank you," said Bulges, handing him the mirror. "Just look into this and tell us what you see."

Putter squinted into the mirror.

"It's hard to tell," he began. "I *do* see something. Yes, I see something. It might be, yes it might be—or rather it could be. No, I would say it couldn't be."

"Couldn't be what?" exclaimed Roundly.

"Couldn't be what I think it is."

"What do you *think* it is?" cried Bulges.

"Either a heap of brush—or a porcupine."

"IT COULDN'T BE!" shouted Bulges and Oddly and Roundly.

At this, Slowly Bear looked up.

"This problem might interest me after all. Maybe I'll try it," he said.

He took the mirror from Putter and placed it under his foot.

"Aren't you going to look into it?" asked Oddly.

Slowly Bear stretched out and closed his eyes.

"All in good time," he said.

"But you can't wait. It's almost dark now!" cried Roundly.

"All the better," muttered Slowly Bear and began to snore.

Putter Porcupine was sensible and went home. But Bulges and Roundly and Oddly waited. They waited while the sun went down. They waited while the moon came up.

And when the moon was up so high that it was hidden by the tops of the tall trees—and the forest was pitch-black dark—they were still waiting.

At last, Slowly Bear woke up. He stretched and puffed and gruffed.

"It's almost time," he said, and took the mirror from under his foot. He looked into it for a long time.

"I knew I could solve this problem," he said at last. "I don't see a thing. Not a single solitary thing."

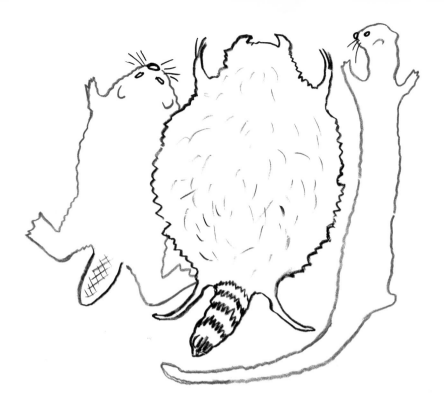

"Are you sure," asked Bulges. "Are you sure you don't see a beaver?"

"Or a raccoon?" asked Roundly.

"Or an otter?" asked Oddly.

"Nothing. Exactly nothing," replied Slowly, handing back the mirror. "Thirty trading stamps, please; that's my usual fee. Of course, if it had taken longer, the charge would be less."

"Longer! That's just the trouble," exclaimed Oddly.

"Yes, you should have looked before it got dark," said Roundly.

"Thirty stamps, please," repeated Slowly.

Bulges had fifteen stamps. Oddly had ten stamps. And Roundly had five.

"Umph," grunted Slowly, taking the thirty stamps and putting them under his foot.

Bulges and Oddly and Roundly said good-by to him and went on their way.

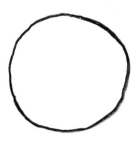

They came to a meadow all silvery with moonlight where Frankly and Bravely Fox were baying at the moon.

"Let's ask them," said Bulges.

The others agreed, so he gave the mirror to the foxes. "Please look into this and tell us what you see," he said.

Frankly and Bravely looked into the mirror.

"It's an ugly old fox," said Frankly.

"It is not. It's a beautiful young fox," said Bravely.

They began to fight.

"You're both wrong," said Bulges, snatching the mirror away from them.

The three friends went off.

By this time, they were rather discouraged.

"I guess we'll never find out," Oddly said.

"Whoo-who, Whoo-who," called Only Owl.

Roundly stopped. "Let's try once more. Let's ask Only Owl," he said.

Roundly took the mirror and climbed up to where Only Owl was perched. "Please look into this and tell us what you see," Roundly said to the owl.

Only Owl flew up toward a higher branch where the light was better.

"What do you see," asked Bulges.

"Whoo-me, Whoo-me," the owl hooted...and dropped the mirror.

CRASH! It fell on a rock below.

Roundly hurried down to the ground.

The mirror had broken into three pieces!

Bulges picked up one of the pieces. "I was right!" he shouted. "It *is* a beaver!"

Roundly picked up another piece. "So was I. It *is* a raccoon!"

Oddly picked up the last piece. She looked and looked. "What a dreamy otter," she said softly.

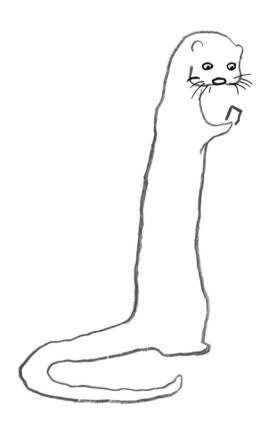

"Whoo-you, Whoo-you," called Only Owl and flew away.